Santa's Secret Gift

Written and Illustrated by
Gary Harbo

Thank you Lord for blessing me with Stephanie Vallin's editing skills

Santa's Secret Gift

Written and Illustrated by
Gary Harbo

Published by KUTIE KARI BOOKS, INC.
Printed in the United States of America,
in North Mankato, Minnesota
062011
20110601

ISBN 978-1-884149-41-2

Copyright © 2011
Kutie Kari Books, Inc.
4189 Ethan Drive, Eagan MN 55123
All rights reserved

Dedicated to my wife...

Barbara Ann Harbo

The Lord put you into my life for a reason. Thanks for all of your support and encouragement, especially during the tough times, which were many. The Lord always gives us more than we deserve, and you are a living example in my life.

On a crisp winter night on the edge of town,
there were two little faces
peeking out a living room window.

They were so excited to see the blanket of snow from the first winter's storm. It was going to be a white Christmas after all.

With only one week left 'til Christmas Eve, there was so much that needed to be done. The family didn't even have their tree yet. But tomorrow was Saturday, and Dad had promised to take the family out to get it.

Grace was so excited that she could hardly wait. Cutting down the Christmas tree was a family tradition, and in her family, traditions were important.

Her little brother Trace was in a rare mood. Normally he was trying to stir up trouble, but tonight he was content to simply watch the snow.

Cut your own Christmas tree

Saturday turned out to be a wonderful day for the drive into the country to find a Christmas tree. They went to the same farm that they always went to, and Mom found a nice tree high up on the hill. They all loved it, so Dad pulled out his saw and began to cut it down. While everyone was watching, they enjoyed a cup of hot chocolate that Mom had brought along in a thermos. Mom always did cool things that warmed them up on the inside.

Dad let them both help pull the tree down the hill. Then it took all of them working together to lift that huge tree up on top of their van. Well, everyone but Trace. He was too busy making the perfect snowball.

Just as Grace turned around she was greeted with a loud thud.

"Trace!" Grace yelled as the snowball thumped her in the chest. "You are a pain."

5

After the drive home, Dad put the tree in the stand. Mom brought all of the decorations up from storage in the basement. She turned the stereo to a station that played Christmas music and made a cup of coffee for herself and Dad. While they sat back and relaxed, Grace and Trace were thrilled to decorate the tree.

"Now it feels like Christmas," Grace exclaimed as she finished hanging the last two bulbs on the tree. "Hey, where did Trace run off to?" she asked Mom and Dad.

"Leave those cats alone!" Mom sternly warned Trace, but it was too late.

The cats had seen Trace sneaking up on them, so Flash quickly leaped onto his back while Tiger began to bat his head like a punching bag.

"Get these cats off me!" Trace screamed as he hid his face in his hands.

Grace couldn't help but laugh as she rescued her brother from his own foolishness.

7

Sunday afternoon Mom took the kids to see Santa at the mall. Dad stayed home to hang the outdoor Christmas lights.

They were so excited. Trace had a long list of toys that he wanted to share with Santa.

"Where is your list, Grace?" Mom asked as she finished reading Trace's second page.

"I don't have one, Mom," Grace replied as she turned and saw Santa motioning her forward.

"Good afternoon young lady," Santa boomed in his jolly voice. "Why don't you come up here and tell Santa what you'd like for Christmas."

She smiled at Santa as he sat down and lifted her up onto his lap.

"Ho, Ho, Ho. What is your name, little girl?" he asked as she looked up at him with her big blue eyes.

9

"My name is Grace, Santa," she eagerly said.

"Grace! That is a beautiful name," Santa smiled in reply.

"It's nothing special," Grace laughed.

"Someday you will know the true power of your name," Santa quietly said, "but today let's find out what you'd like for Christmas."

"I'll tell you what I'd like for Christmas, Santa," Grace said as she broke out into a big grin, "but only if you promise to tell me what you want for Christmas."

"Well, I have never heard of such a thing," Santa said as he chuckled to himself. "Christmas is for children, Grace. Now please tell me what you would like."

11

"Well, I love to paint and draw, Santa, so I'd like to get a set of paints and maybe a paint-by-number picture," Grace said with a sparkle in her eye.

"I can tell that you are the creative type," Santa's voice boomed again. "I think that is an excellent choice!"

"Okay, Santa, now it's your turn," Grace said with a grin.

"Grace, I'm honored that you want to know what I would like for Christmas," Santa spoke in a quiet voice. "but I actually received my perfect gift many years ago. In fact, I was just a few years older than you are now."

"Really, Santa?" Grace asked. "Please tell me what that gift was."

"Well, this is quite unusual, Grace. But I can tell that you are an unusual girl, so I'm going to grant your request on one condition."

"What is that Santa?" Grace said.

"That you keep this secret until you understand what it truly means." And as Grace nodded her head, Santa whispered the secret into her ear. Before Grace could ask another question, Santa set her on the floor and Trace quickly leaped onto his lap.

13